# BECOMING
# PRINCE
# CHARMING

# SUDDENLY ROYAL

# BECOMING PRINCE CHARMING

LOREN BAILEY

MINNEAPOLIS

Darby Creek
A division of Lerner Publishing Group, Inc.
241 First Avenue North
Minneapolis, MN 55401  USA

For reading levels and more information, look up this title at
www.lernerbooks.com.

Cover and interior images: Igor Klimov/Shutterstock.com (background texture); GoMixer/Shutterstock.com (coat of arms and lion); KazanovskyAndrey/iStock/Getty Images Plus (gold); mona redshinestudio/Shutterstock.com (crown).

Main body text set in Janson Text LT Std 12/17.5.
Typeface provided by Adobe Systems.

**Library of Congress Cataloging-in-Publication Data**

Names: Bailey, Loren, author.
Title: Becoming Prince Charming / Loren Bailey.
Description: Minneapolis : Darby Creek, [2018] | Series: Suddenly royal | Summary: On his seventeenth birthday, slacker Mason learns his absentee mother is a member of the Evonian royal family and, with a little hard work, his life as a royal could be more interesting than video games. | Identifiers: LCCN 2017049271 (print) | LCCN 2017059831 (ebook) | ISBN 9781541525931 (eb pdf) | ISBN 9781541525702 (lb : alk. paper) | ISBN 9781541526365 (pb : alk. paper)
Subjects: | CYAC: Countesses—Fiction. | Mothers and sons—Fiction. | Conduct of life—Fiction. | Friendship—Fiction. | Europe—Fiction.
Classification: LCC PZ7.1.B326 (ebook) | LCC PZ7.1.B326 Bec 2018 (print) | DDC [Fic]—dc23

LC record available at https://lccn.loc.gov/2017049271

Manufactured in the United States of America
1-44554-35485-2/16/2018

To Mitch—I'm forever grateful
for all the love and support

# The Valmont Family of Evonia

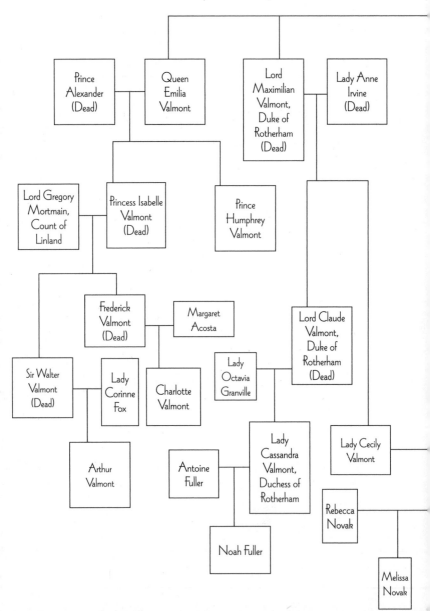

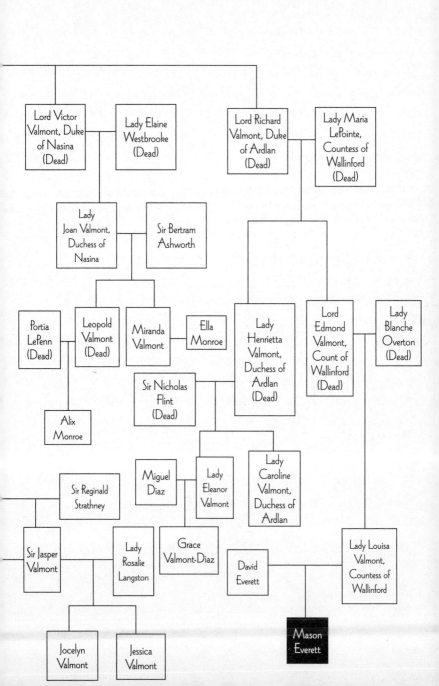

1

*Our team will need a couple hundred more points if we want to win this thing.* Mason Everett checked the countdown clock on the wall— only thirty seconds left to go. He crouched behind a neon block, eyes scanning the black splatter-painted walls for any sign of the opposing team.

In the distance, he heard a blast and a shout of frustration from his friend Andre. With the amount of time it took to recharge after a hit, Mason knew Andre was basically out at this point. He had no idea how Chase, their other teammate, was doing.

Mason spotted a flash of blue. He darted to another neon structure and peered through a small peephole. Three of the blue team's members were clustered inside a tall tower of painted plywood. *Must be trying to ride out the clock*, Mason thought to himself. If he could get all three of them, there was a good chance that his team would win.

Fifteen seconds on the clock. It was now or never.

He slipped out of his hiding place and jogged over to the tower. His footsteps gave him away. One of the blue team members looked over and spotted him. He gasped, and all of Mason's targets raced away in different directions.

"Go, Mason, go!" Chase shouted to him from across the arena. But Mason felt himself hesitate. These players weren't sitting ducks anymore—he'd have to sprint after one just for the chance that he *might* hit him.

"It's pointless," he said, as the clock counted off the last three seconds.

"Whatever, Mason," Andre grumbled as a loud buzzer went off. "You still could have tried."

Chase joined them, panting. "Please. Have you ever heard the words 'Mason' and 'try' in the same sentence?"

"Yeah, here's one for you: I'll try not to smack you," Mason snapped. "And hey, aren't you supposed to be nice to a guy on his birthday?"

"Yeah, as long as he helps you win at laser tag," Chase joked.

They made their way out of the arena, pulling off their orange chest plates. As they hung their gear on the designated hooks, a large screen displayed the teams' statistics:

BLUE TEAM: 3,200 POINTS

ORANGE TEAM: 3,050 POINTS

CONGRATULATIONS, BLUE TEAM!

His friends sighed at the screen and Mason tried to pretend he didn't notice. It was just laser tag. Who really cared?

"Fine, sorry or whatever. Can we go now?" he grumbled.

It was no secret that Mason wasn't exactly

the type to take initiative, but neither were his friends. It's why they were friends in the first place. They spent their days sitting in the back rows of classrooms, trying to go unnoticed by teachers as they doodled cartoons on their desks and worked to get past the school's website blockers.

Mason and his friends trudged out of the laser tag arena, stopping by the arcade's concession stand for one last round of nachos and sodas before heading home. As far as he was concerned, it was the perfect way to celebrate his seventeenth birthday.

He told himself to ignore the needling guilt in the back of his mind, where his friends' words kept bouncing around. They weren't disappointed in him, not really. And even if they were, they'd get over it soon enough.

\*\*\*

Most of the lights in the house were out when Mason got home. It was late, so he figured his dad had already gone to bed. He was about to slip upstairs into his own bedroom when he spotted his dad sitting at the kitchen table.

"Uh, Dad?" Mason said quietly, stepping into the room. "Everything okay?"

His dad looked up at him with a tight smile. "Hey, bud," he said, rubbing at his eyes. "Happy birthday. Did you guys have fun?"

"Yeah . . . what's going on?" As Mason stepped closer to his dad, he saw there were dozens of papers strewn across the table.

"Why don't you sit down?" his dad suggested. "We need to talk."

Had he done something? Nothing came to mind. Sure, he and his friends liked to goof around, but they usually didn't get into the kind of trouble that led to a sit-down with his dad.

He slid into the chair across from his dad, and the room was silent for a minute. Mason didn't dare look down at the papers to see if he could get any sort of clue from them—all he could do was stare at his dad's face and the frown lines forming there. His dad was still pretty young—he'd just turned forty a few months ago—but in this moment he looked much older than Mason had ever seen.

"I want—" his dad started, then shook his head. "I need to tell you about your mother."

"Oh." Mason definitely hadn't expected the conversation to go this way. He knew very little about his mother, but he'd always figured that was because there wasn't much to tell. He knew she and his dad were young when they met and had Mason, and that things didn't end well—he didn't need his dad to tell him that part. He figured that since they never spoke about her, things must have been bad. He'd seen enough friends deal with messy custody battles and difficult family drama that he'd decided he'd rather not know.

His dad gathered several of the papers on the table, pulled them into a cluttered pile, and handed them to Mason.

"Emails?" Mason asked when he glanced at them. "Dad, what's going on?"

"These are printouts of email conversations I've been having with your mother," his dad explained slowly. Mason felt the pages drop out of his hands. One of them shifted to show a conversation dated from five years ago.

"You've been talking to her? But I thought . . . For how long?" Suddenly there were too many questions racing through his mind. Mason couldn't get them all out at once.

"We never really lost contact. It was more difficult right after you were born, but we've been speaking regularly over the past few years now."

"*What?*" Mason snapped. "And you never felt the need to tell me?"

"I couldn't," his dad insisted. "Or, at least, I thought I couldn't. It's what we agreed on. And now . . . well, just let me tell you everything."

Mason angrily waved a hand in his dad's direction and slumped back in his seat. "Go ahead."

His dad licked his lips and took another deep breath. He kept his eyes down as he began, "You already know some of this—I met your mother when I was in my early twenties. I'd just graduated from college and was traveling the country for the summer before I was going to buckle down and get a job. I met her somewhere along the way. She was doing the same thing."

Mason nodded. While he admittedly didn't know much about the situation, his dad had mentioned a few snippets over the years.

"We hit it off instantly," his dad continued. "I'd never met someone like her—we fell in love. And then, before we really had a chance to talk about plans for the future, she got pregnant with you."

When his dad finally looked up at him, Mason was surprised to see the guilt in his eyes—he'd never seen his dad look like that before. "We made some fast decisions because we were worried about what her family would think. We decided to get married and tell everyone you were planned. We moved here, and things were fine for a while. But soon it became clear we didn't actually know each other that well. We tried to make it work for a few months after you were born, but we just couldn't do it. We were too different."

"So you got divorced," Mason finished. He'd already known that part too. "But here's what I don't get: Why couldn't she still have stayed around? Why keep all the secrets? Didn't she want to know me?"

His dad looked at him with pained eyes. "Of course she wanted to know you. But it wasn't that simple."

Mason could tell there was something his dad was leaving out. He raised his eyebrows expectantly.

"Well, your mom wasn't—she isn't American actually. She's European. From a country called Evonia."

"What?" Mason frowned. "I've never even heard of it."

His dad sighed. "It's a small country."

Mason's head began to pound. He could barely comprehend what he was hearing. He looked back down at the papers in front of him and noticed a name. "Louisa. Louisa Valmont." He glanced up at his dad. "That's her?"

His dad nodded again. "I should have told you about her sooner. I wish that I had."

"I still don't understand," Mason said.

His dad picked up one of the papers and handed it to him. This time, Mason took a closer look at the actual document. There was a fancy crest at the bottom of each of Louisa's email signatures, along with her full name: Lady Louisa Valmont, Countess of Wallinford.

"We thought keeping you here with me would be the best thing for you," his dad explained, "especially since your birth was sort of scandalous in her social circles. And her parents . . . well, that doesn't matter now. The point is it's time I told you—not only is your mother from another country, she's a countess. She's a member of Evonia's royal family."

Mason's jaw dropped. He certainly hadn't seen that coming.

"And that's not all," his dad continued. "As her only child, you're next in line to inherit her title."

His dad continued explaining it as best as he could—that Louisa's parents thought it would be best for her to return to Evonia since there was no one else in place to take her mother's title. So she did, and shortly after her return, her mother passed away. Louisa became a countess, and Mason's parents never spoke about her returning to America again. Her branch of the family wasn't directly in line for the throne, but she was a royal nonetheless. She was related to Evonia's queen. Mason was related to Evonia's queen. He still could barely wrap his head around the idea.

Since his dad hadn't wanted to move to Evonia, his parents had faced a tough decision about how Mason would be raised. In the end, they agreed the simplest plan would be for Mason to grow up away from the public eye and avoid having to travel between countries every year. Their plan was that Mason would live with his dad until he turned eighteen, then he would go to Evonia to meet Louisa.

But now his dad was beginning to question their arrangement. "I was only twenty-three," he explained. "We were panicking—we didn't know anyone who'd been in a situation like this before. We did what we thought was best. Throughout the years, though, it's become more and more difficult to keep this from you. Seeing you become your own person, so independent, I just had to do something."

He paused for a moment. "Your—Louisa doesn't know about this. She still thinks I'm planning to wait to tell you until you turn eighteen. I just wanted to give you some time to think about it before you have to decide if you'd like to see her next year."

"What does she think about all of this?" Mason asked.

"It's been difficult for her too," his dad insisted. "More so, in some ways. But she's gone along with it this whole time because she truly believed it's best for you."

"Does she know anything about me?"

"A little. We email a few times a year, as you can see from these printouts. I've sent her things occasionally—photos, report cards."

Mason flushed at that. While he'd never cared about his grades or lack of after-school activities before, he couldn't help but worry about what his mother had thought. He wondered how his dad had explained it: *"It's not that Mason isn't good at anything, he just doesn't care."* It sounded worse when he thought about it like that, so he tried not to think about it at all.

Completely overwhelmed and wanting to be alone, Mason went to bed. But a half hour later, he was lying awake, unable to *stop* thinking about his mom. He was angry— downright pissed off—that his parents had made what seemed like such an incredibly stupid decision. But he also couldn't stop himself from wondering about her—what did she look like, what did her voice sound like, how much time had she spent with him when he was a baby?

Mason's fingers twitched against his head, and he held out for one more minute before scrambling out of bed and opening his laptop. He pulled up a search and typed in his mom's full name.

It was surprising to see how many hits the search called up.

There were quite a few European articles about Louisa and her family—even some from the United States. Most were about some foundation she'd started. Mason found the website for the foundation, which was dedicated to children's health research. Not that Mason knew much about foundations, but hers seemed pretty impressive. It looked like she worked hard to raise money through charity events and other fundraising. He found a page filled with event photos and scrolled through them. Most of them were of children the foundation had supported. Some donors and volunteers. A silent auction fundraising event.

He was clicking through the photos so mindlessly that he actually jumped when he came across a photo of a woman posing with a group of kids and saw the caption beneath: "Lady Louisa Valmont, founder and Chairperson of the Board, with several attendants of last year's annual Children's Dinner."

It was a small photo. The image of Louisa's head was barely larger than his thumb. But Mason could clearly see himself in her. She had long brown hair, darker than his, but it was clear that they had the same square facial structure. Her eyes were slightly different than his, but he found himself trying to remember if his creased in the same way when he smiled.

His heart pounded in his chest as he stared at her picture. He didn't know what he was expecting her to look like, but something about her already seemed so familiar.

He searched through the menu at the top of the page and found an "About" section. There was a page dedicated entirely to Louisa. The bio didn't give much information—mostly just details about her schooling, her work as the

Countess of Wallinford, and how she began the foundation. What stood out the most to Mason, though, was the fact that there was no mention of her ever remarrying or having another family.

***

The next morning, Mason woke up early to catch his dad before work. He found him skimming through several of the printed emails while sipping coffee.

"Morning," his dad said hesitantly, clearly trying to guess how Mason was doing.

But Mason was ready to get right down to it. "I want to meet her," he said. His dad opened his mouth to reply, but Mason carried on. "I still think what you guys did was stupid—and I'm still super pissed about it. But she's my mom and I want to meet her."

After a moment of thinking, his dad nodded. "Okay. We can—"

"And I don't want to wait till I'm eighteen," Mason continued. "I don't even get where you guys came up with that number anyway." *As if turning eighteen would magically make me ready to meet the mother I never knew about*, he thought to himself.

His dad scratched the back of his neck. "Well, I don't even really remember, to be honest. I guess we figured you'd be old enough to understand the situation better—how things were different for us because of who Louisa is."

Before Mason could respond, his dad coughed nervously and fiddled with one of the pages in front of him. "And, I think Louisa has been thinking you might want to make some decisions about college . . . career stuff . . . whether you want to take up her title when the time comes."

That caught Mason off guard. *Is that what this visit is supposed to be about? Am I gonna get sucked into this job without even knowing what it is?*

His dad seemed to sense Mason's mind reeling and lifted a calming hand toward him. "You don't have to do anything you don't want to," he explained. "That's not what this is about. She just wants to meet you."

Mason let out a long breath. "Okay." He sat at the table and leaned back in his seat, staring into space as he tried to process even more new information. His dad sat down as well and patiently waited for Mason to speak again.

"I think I still want to go. Before I even think about taking her title, I want to meet her. See the country. That kind of stuff."

His dad nodded again.

"And I wanna go now. This summer."

His dad looked at him in surprise. "I'll see what I can do."

3

One week later, Mason and his dad were on a flight to France. Evonia didn't have its own airport, so Louisa had arranged for a car to pick them up and drive them into the country. They were staying for an entire month, so Mason and Louisa would have plenty of time to get to know each other.

Mason wasn't sure exactly what he was expecting, but he was surprised to see a driver dressed in a black suit waiting for them at the airport with his name on a little sign. He'd never had a professional driver before—or ridden in a fancy town car. If nothing else, this would at least be the most interesting trip he'd ever taken.

The driver didn't say much to them as he drove over the border into Evonia, and Mason and his dad spent most of the car ride looking out the windows in the back seat. Overall, the rural landscape looked pretty similar to what Mason was used to seeing in the US. It wasn't until they drove into Louisa's hometown that Mason began to notice the subtle differences. People's clothes were slightly different. Cars looked slightly different. All of the signs were in English, but many of them also showed French and German translations.

"Is English their main language?" Mason asked, keeping his gaze out the window.

"I think so, yeah," his dad said. "But I think many people here are also fluent in French and German. Your . . . Louisa is, if I remember right."

"What else do you know about Evonia?"

His dad blew a puff of air out of his mouth. "Not much. I've never been here before."

Mason looked at his dad in shock. "Really?"

His dad shrugged. "We weren't even together for that long. And by the time she got pregnant, I don't think her parents were too crazy about me."

"Did you ever meet them?"

"No, but I'd heard a little about them from Louisa."

His dad's parents had both passed away when Mason was little. Aside from some cousins, aunts, and uncles on his dad's side who he saw every few years, Mason didn't have much in terms of extended family. It was weird to think there would be this new person to add. He knew both of his mom's parents had passed away, but he wondered if she had any other living relatives.

Before he could ask, the car pulled up to a tall set of wrought-iron gates. The driver spoke their names into an intercom, and moments later the gates swung open. The house was huge, covered in tan brick and dozens of windows. It was situated in the center of a large plot of land, filled with rolling grassy hills and the occasional tree. Mason had never seen a house like this before. He could hardly believe his mother lived here. Did that mean this house was technically his too? He felt dizzy just thinking about it.

Mason rolled down the window a bit, trying to breathe in some fresh air. The car stopped in front of the house. He wiped his sweaty palms against his jeans.

"All right," his dad said, unbuckling his seatbelt. "Here we go."

***

A woman at the front door introduced herself as the housekeeper. She smiled warmly at them but didn't give much information before she turned to lead them through the house. Mason left his bags near the front door, taking in the sights of the house.

It was impossibly clean. It was hard to believe anyone actually lived here. The floors and stairs were marble, and practically everything else was covered in dark wood. Several family paintings and photos lined the walls—most of them showing an elderly couple and a woman Mason recognized as Louisa throughout the years. He wondered if he'd ever have a picture hanging on these walls.

The housekeeper brought them to a set of French doors in the back of the house, revealing a lush garden just outside. Mason paused, noticing his dad had stopped. "Dad?"

His dad gave him a reassuring smile and leaned against the doorframe. "Go on—I'll be right over here."

Mason tried to return the smile but could feel the nerves growing. His heart began to pound, and he took one last deep breath. Mason nodded and continued on by himself. As he stepped outside, he spotted a small table and chairs, where a woman was waiting.

"Hello, Mason," she said, giving him a soft smile. "I'm Louisa."

4

"Please," Louisa said, gesturing to the chair beside her, "take a seat."

Mason swallowed heavily. The last time a parent had asked him to do that, he learned he was royalty. He wondered what bomb might get dropped during this conversation.

He sat down anyway, noticing the way Louisa primly lowered herself into her chair after he did. She smiled nervously at him again. "It's so nice to meet you . . . well, see you."

He was surprised to realize she spoke with a slight accent.

"Yeah, I, uh, know what you mean," Mason said. He tried to give a smile back, and Louisa let out a breathy laugh. Her hand fluttered at her collarbone and she reached for one of the glasses of water sitting on the table, taking a long drink.

"I'm sorry," she said. "I didn't think I would be this nervous when the time came."

Mason nodded.

"Perhaps we should start from the beginning," Louisa started, sitting up straighter and clearing her throat like she was about to interview him. "How is school going?"

*Kind of a weird place to start*, thought Mason. And school wasn't something he particularly enjoyed speaking about. "It's fine, I guess. I have good friends there."

She nodded. "And classes?"

He shrugged. Louisa cleared her throat again and gave him what he guessed she hoped was a reassuring smile. "I only ask because, as you know, part of the reason we wanted to bring you here was so you could consider taking on my title eventually. And schooling would be very important for that aspect, so—"

"Wait a minute." Mason sat up. "What do you mean 'as I know'?"

Her eyes darted over to where his dad was still standing by the house, and Mason was able to put it all together. "Dad told you what we talked about on my birthday?"

Before Louisa could answer, Mason's dad walked over. "Hello, Louisa. How are—"

Mason cut him off. "You two were emailing even after we had that talk?"

"Mason," his dad said, looking surprised, "you knew I was in touch with Louisa to get this set up."

"Yeah, but I thought it was just, like, making travel plans. I didn't realize you were still talking about me." He flushed at the idea of the two of them discussing him. What had his dad told her? And, more importantly—

"Why didn't I get to talk with her over these past few weeks?" he asked. "We could have at least emailed or something."

"Mason," Louisa started, "we just thought—"

"So once again you made a decision about me without me," he interrupted. "Even though it affects me more than either of you."

"That's not what we were trying to do," his dad insisted.

Mason turned to Louisa. "And what is this to you? A job interview? You're meeting me for the first time since I was a baby and the first thing you ask me is if I have good enough grades to take over your job some day?"

Louisa's eyes went wide. "I didn't mean it that way."

"How about I get to try an interview question now? Here's one: why did you leave me?"

"Mason—"

"I could have spent my summers here or something. Couldn't you have at least visited me?"

Louisa stared at him for a moment. "It's not that simple. I had obligations, responsibilities that I couldn't just leave behind. And," she tucked her hair behind her ears nervously, "there were some who believed it would be better not to call attention to you or David— er, your dad."

"What?" Mason said. "So you cut us out

of your life entirely because you were afraid of what people might think about you?"

"No, that's not what I meant," she said hastily. She took a deep breath. "Listen, Mason, what you have to understand is that my family—my parents especially—were very strict. They were . . . rather old-fashioned in their ways."

Mason frowned. "So, what, your *family* didn't want you to have me?"

"I—well, I think they just would have preferred if I'd been married here and settled down first . . ."

"So my own grandparents didn't want me, and because they told you to abandon me, you did."

"No, of course not. There's more to it than that—"

He stood quickly, his chair scraping against the ground. "I think I'm done talking now."

"Mason, wait—"

He walked past his dad back into the house, not knowing where he was going but not really caring either. He clomped up the stairs

and found a bedroom that had his suitcase
waiting inside.

Mason slammed the door closed behind
him, not caring that he was in somebody else's
house. Especially since that somebody was
supposed to be his mother and instead was a
total stranger.

*Screw the plan*, he thought to himself
angrily. He'd had enough already. He was ready
to go home.

\*\*\*

Mason was left alone for about an hour before
he heard a soft knock on his door. Figuring
it was his dad, Mason was surprised to see
Louisa standing on the other side of the door.
He didn't know what to do other than stare
at her.

"Could I come in?" she asked quietly.

He stepped away from the door, pushing
it open in invitation as he sat back down on
the bed. Louisa glanced around and eyed the
desk chair at the other side of the room before
sitting at the foot of the bed instead.

"Mason." She looked him squarely in the eye, and Mason forced himself not to look away. But he also felt sort of amused at her obvious determination and wanted to see where she would go with this. "I want to apologize for what happened in the garden."

Then she did something else Mason wasn't expecting—she began to laugh. She lowered her face into her hands, letting her hair fall in a curtain around her. "I can't believe you've only been here for an hour and I already have to apologize for my behavior. This didn't go at all the way I had planned."

"I guess this is kind of weird and new for both of us."

Louisa looked up at him and gave what looked like the first genuine smile he'd seen from her since he arrived. "Look, I know I've made a lot of mistakes—it's going to take me a long time to get this right. But I want to try. I want to make things right."

He nodded.

"How about we start over?" She brushed her hair away from her face and straightened up. "It's just about time for dinner. We can sit down together with your dad. I'd love to hear all about your life—your friends, your hobbies, anything you want to tell me about."

"Um, okay," Mason said. "Yeah. I'd like that."

Over the next few days, Mason felt like he was living in a movie. He got to wake up whenever he wanted, then he'd go downstairs where he could order anything he wanted for breakfast from the kitchen staff. Once Louisa found out he was into video games, she had a large TV and game console set up for him in his bedroom. The better Mason got to know the household staff, the easier it became to ask them for other things—a mini fridge, a cell phone on an Evonian plan, a huge speaker system, any video game he could think of. He ate meals with his parents, which involved a lot of awkwardly polite conversations, but the rest of the time he could do whatever he wanted.

But on Friday, the dream ended.

"A party?" Mason mumbled through a mouthful of French toast.

Louisa nodded, taking a sip of tea as she scrolled through the news on her tablet. "Mhmm, it's being thrown by Lord Pembrooke—he works with me on the foundation."

Mason could feel the deep frown growing on his face. "So this is gonna be some boring, fancy thing?"

"Not at all, it will be fun!" Louisa assured, grinning at him. She glanced at his dad, seated across from her at the breakfast table, as if he needed to be convinced too. "It will mostly be people I work with and from my social circles, yes, but I can assure you, we know how to have a good time."

Mason eyed her, feeling almost positive this would be an event with snooty people talking about politics and other things he didn't care about. He'd probably have to wear a suit.

Just as he was about to open his mouth and tell her "Thanks but no thanks," his dad glanced over at him and said, "I'm sure Mason would be happy to go along. Especially considering all the nice gifts you've given him lately, which he's incredibly thankful for."

*Oh, you've got to be kidding me*, Mason thought. He could hear his dad's message loud and clear: go to the boring stuff Louisa wants to drag you to or you lose your new toys. He huffed and shoveled another piece of French toast into his mouth.

"Okay, I'll go."

Louisa beamed at that. "This will be so much fun, Mason, trust me. We'll have a *great* time!"

"What are you planning to tell people about Mason?" his dad asked, sipping his coffee. "Will that cause some . . . issues?"

"Well, we won't do any sort of formal announcement, no, but if anyone asks we'll tell them he's my son," Louisa explained. "I doubt many people will ask, though. Most of them probably already know the situation—you'd be surprised at how much these people love their gossip."

Mason sighed. He was definitely going to have to wear a suit.

***

That night, a car pulled up to the front of the house to pick them up. Mason followed Louisa outside, yanking at the tie around his neck.

"Stop fidgeting," his dad said, swatting Mason's hands away and re-straightening the tie.

Mason stuffed his hands into his pockets. "Are you sure you can't come too?" he asked.

"This trip is about you and Louisa getting to know each other."

"Yeah, yeah."

His dad gave him a reassuring smile, clasping his shoulders. "You'll be fine."

Mason sighed. At least if his dad came along he'd have someone to make fun of all the snobby people with.

The car ride was pretty quiet. Every few minutes Louisa would mention someone who would be there tonight. But there were too many names and references for him to keep track of, so he turned his attention to staring outside the window, already counting down the hours till this night would be over.

They arrived at the house—another fancy mansion on a large plot of land. A few people were gathered in small groups outside, but the majority of the guests were inside in the mansion's banquet hall.

It was exactly as Mason had expected.

Everyone was dressed in ball gowns and tuxedos. A string quartet played classical music in the corner. Wait staff carried around trays of champagne and tiny appetizers. Mason figured there had to be a fountain somewhere.

A group immediately waved Louisa over, and Mason trailed slowly behind her. He was prepared to stand off to the side, when Louisa turned suddenly and placed a hand on his back.

"Everyone, I'd like you to meet my son, Mason," she said proudly. This wasn't what Mason had expected based on his parents' earlier conversation. Before Mason could reflect too much on that, the crowd of people began speaking all at once—asking him how he was enjoying his visit to Evonia and how long he was planning to stay. As Louisa had guessed this morning, they clearly already knew the story around his birth and why he was here now.

Louisa introduced everyone by name, but she also included their titles. It was impossible to keep straight—there was Lord Whatshisface and Sir So-and-So and the Duchess of Something-or-Other. Apparently everyone at this party was a noble.

Mason listened to Louisa and Lord Whatshisface talk about a conference they were going to for about a half hour before he decided he couldn't stand another moment of small talk. Finally, there was a pause in the conversation and he decided to make a break for it.

"Um—" He didn't know what to call her. Lady Louisa? Ma'am? "Mom" didn't seem right yet. "Louisa?" he said quietly, not sure what the high society rule was for what you were supposed to publicly call the woman who birthed you but you didn't really know.

She stepped away and looked at him expectantly.

"Is it cool if I get something to eat?"

"Oh, of course!" Louisa said, looking upset with herself for not realizing he might be hungry. "Go ahead. I'll find you later."

As soon as he stepped away, he tugged his tie loose and undid the top button of his dress shirt. At least that was a little better. And hey, he'd managed to keep the tie in place for an hour. That had to count for something.

The food the wait staff had on their trays wasn't very appealing. He was craving a burger and some chili cheese fries, but so far all he'd come across were tiny pieces of cheese, a platter of weird Evonian fruit, and what Mason was fairly certain were fish eggs. The cheese was fine and the fruits were mostly like weird raisins and pears, but none of it was actually very filling.

"Doesn't anyone actually eat at these things?" Mason muttered to himself, wondering if it would look bad if he took off his suit jacket.

"Not much," a voice laughed.

He was surprised—the voice sounded like it came from someone his own age. Mason turned around to see a guy and girl standing off to the side together.

"You guys someone's kids?" he asked.

"I'm Nathan Beaumont," the boy said, then gestured to the girl. "And this is Cora Kensington." She gave a friendly wave.

"I'm Mason," he said. Then, because he felt like he needed to, quickly added, "Everett."

"Our parents drag us to these things all the time," Cora explained, rolling her eyes jokingly. By the way Nathan touched her lower back, Mason guessed that they didn't actually mind being here together.

Speaking with the same light accent as Louisa, they explained who each of their parents were, and Mason didn't bother pretending he recognized them.

A waiter approached them and asked a question, but it was in French and Mason didn't understand a word of it. Nathan and Cora responded in French, then turned to him. Mason felt his face flush as they slowly came to realize he didn't speak French.

"He just wants to know if we want anything to drink. What would you like? Soda? Tea?"

"Oh, ah, I'll just have a root beer," Mason said, looking between Cora and the waiter. He waited for Cora to translate, but the waiter just nodded and stepped away.

"Jeez, does everyone speak three languages here?" he asked.

"So you *aren't* from here," Cora said excitedly, as Nathan elbowed her. She bit her lip and shrugged at him.

Nathan turned to Mason and tried to laugh lightheartedly. "We *may* have heard that Louisa Valmont's son from America was coming to visit."

Mason raised his eyebrows. "So do you all know the whole story already?"

"Not much," Cora admitted. "Just the basics." She shared a glance with Nathan again and hastily added, "We haven't said anything—we've just heard some talk."

"We didn't recognize you, and like we said, we go to all these things, so we kind of guessed who you were," Nathan explained.

To Mason's relief, they didn't press him for details. Instead, they spent the rest of the evening introducing him to Evonian soda, teaching him enough French to talk a waiter into bringing him a sandwich from the kitchen, and starting a betting pool on which of the old people would fall asleep in their seats first. He learned that Nathan played guitar for a local band and that Nathan and Cora had been dating for a little over a year now. For the first time all night, Mason was actually enjoying himself.

Nathan was telling him about his favorite Evonian bands that Mason would have to check out when Cora waved to someone.

"Oh, there's Brianna!" she said, touching Nathan's elbow. "I'll bring her over to say hello."

"Brianna is Lord Pembrooke's daughter," Nathan explained. He pointed to a man across the room—Lord Whatshisface, Mason realized—the guy throwing the party.

**6**

Mason assumed that Brianna Pembrooke would be like all the other gorgeous popular girls he went to school with—the girls who knew how attractive they were and used it to get whatever they wanted. So he fully expected to get a little smile from Brianna when Cora brought her over and then some half-baked excuse as to why she would have to walk away nearly immediately.

But instead, she gave a relieved sigh when Nathan offered her a sip of his soda.

"I haven't been able to eat all night," Brianna said with a groan, raising one foot out of her high heel to rub it. "My dad has been dragging me around to say hi to everyone this whole time, and all I've been thinking about is how much I want something smothered in cheese."

Mason raised his eyebrows at that. "If, uh, you find anything, you should let me know."

Brianna looked over, staring at him for a second before bursting into laughter. "Where did you guys find *him*?" she asked.

"He's Louisa Valmont's son," Nathan explained.

Understanding dawned on Brianna's face and she looked him up and down. "The infamous American son. We'd heard you were coming into town."

Mason felt himself flush a bit under her gaze. "Uh, yeah. Well, here I am."

And just like that, Brianna and Cora turned their attention from Mason to start their own conversation. For a moment, he couldn't help but stare at Brianna. He barely knew her, but already there was something about her. Something he'd never noticed in another girl before . . .

He cut off that train of thought and glanced

at Nathan. "So, what else do you guys do around here besides have fancy parties and talk about scandalous American children?"

Nathan laughed. "Well, I have two more years of school. And other than my band, I usually spend most of my time volunteering in one of our forest preserves."

"Really?" Mason asked. "Is that, like, something your school makes you do?"

"Not exactly. I want to become a vet and work for our national wildlife program," Nathan explained. "So I'm trying to get some more experience before I apply to universities."

Mason took a long drink from his root beer. "Oh, right. So that's big around here too, huh."

"What do you mean?"

He shrugged. "Having some kind of 'master plan' for your life."

Nathan frowned. "You say that like it's a bad thing."

"I'm just saying, you have your whole life ahead of you. Why do you have to map it all out now? You still have time."

"Maybe," Nathan said. He gestured toward the girls. "But Cora will take over her family title someday. She's basically had to prepare for that her entire life. And Brianna wants to start a foundation like Louisa's. She'll need to get a lot of experience first."

The girls smiled as they listened to Nathan list off their plans, as if they were genuinely excited about their futures. Mason blinked at them. "Really?"

"Yeah." Cora nodded. "I want to work around the country to get to know it better— maybe learn about our government a little more. Right now I have a part-time job working at city hall."

"And I'll probably study business and get several years of work experience before I even consider getting my own foundation off the ground," Brianna added. "But for now I've been doing some volunteering, and I'll probably do a few internships while I'm in school."

"Don't you do something besides go to school?" Nathan asked Mason.

"I, uh . . . my friends and I hang out at our skate park most of the time," Mason said. The others just looked at him. He coughed. "And, um, sometimes I help my dad around the house. It can be a lot of work. I have to, like, mow the lawn. Take out the garbage."

Nathan, Cora, and Brianna just gave him polite smiles.

"Sure, it's important to help your family and take care of your home," Nathan said.

Mason tried not to cringe in embarrassment. He reminded himself that people who planned out their whole lives in advance didn't have much fun. *They* were the followers, while he was the one who would have freedom for the rest of his life. *They're just blind to the system that's keeping them trapped in predictable lives*, he reassured himself. *I should feel sorry for them.*

"Whatever," Mason said then. "I'm not gonna let myself get tricked into doing something I don't want to do just because I think I'm supposed to do it. I'd rather live my life one day at a time."

The others looked stunned at this. They stared at him for a moment as if barely able to process what he'd said. Then they each gave him empty smiles.

"Well, good for you, Mason," Brianna said lightly. "At least you're happy with your decision. That's all that matters."

Nathan and Cora nodded quickly—too quickly. They changed the subject to something else, but Mason kept quiet for a bit. He didn't know why, but he suddenly felt off. He was used to people judging him for not wanting to do anything after high school, but, for the first time, Mason couldn't help but wonder if he was actually making the right choice for himself.

\*\*\*

It wasn't until nearly midnight that the party began to slow down. Mason couldn't believe how late these nobles liked to party. Cora and Brianna had taken off their heels at some point during the night, and now they attempted to stuff their feet back into the shoes before their parents noticed they'd been barefoot in front of half the Evonian nobility.

Brianna nearly tumbled over when one of her feet missed her shoe, and she burst into laughter as she suddenly grabbed Mason's shoulder for support. His stomach jumped but he tried to hold still as she leaned on him. She had a nice laugh—carefree. It was the kind of laugh that came right from her belly, like she didn't care about trying to hold it in for appearances.

After she stepped away, Mason cleared his throat. Stuffing his hands into his pockets, he attempted a casual glance toward Nathan. "So, ah," he started, "about Brianna . . ."

Nathan laughed, seeing right through him. "Sorry, mate, but I wouldn't bother—Brianna doesn't exactly go for guys like you."

"What's that supposed to mean?"

"Nothing—just, she usually goes for guys with some . . . ambition."

Mason grumbled to himself, but then he realized Nathan probably had a point. Brianna had been friendly to him all night—she

laughed at his jokes and genuinely listened
to him when he spoke—but she hadn't shown
actual interest in him. Not like that.

He sighed and decided to leave it alone for
now. Louisa found him near the front door,
looking exhausted. Mason said goodbye to his
new friends, who all made him swear that he
would keep in touch while he was still in town,
before heading out to the car.

On the ride home, Mason told Louisa
about meeting Nathan, Cora, and Brianna. It
was surprising—Mason had thought he'd get
at least some obvious stares or maybe even
the cold shoulder from people at this party.
But, so far, everyone had been rather relaxed
about it. Maybe his backstory didn't seem as
scandalous to Evonian high society now that
it was old news.

"I'm so glad you had a good time," Louisa
breathed, leaning back in her seat. She
stretched her legs in front of her and pulled
the earrings out of her ears. "To be honest, I
actually don't think these things are half as fun
as I made them out to be. But it's expected that

I go, and I didn't want to scare you away before you even got there."

Mason laughed at that. He liked this relaxed side of Louisa. It was as if he was finally getting to see the real her. "I'm kinda surprised I had fun too. I'm glad I went."

7

Two days later, Mason was attempting to beat
his high score in his new favorite Evonian
racing game when Louisa knocked on the
door. He kept the race going but grunted that
she could come in.

"I have something to show you!" she said,
waving her tablet in her hand. She held it up
to show him something on the screen, but
Mason couldn't tell what it said from where he
was sitting. When he didn't react, she loudly
cleared her throat.

He sighed and paused the game, turning to
look at her.

"The foundation is hosting another event
next week—an ice cream social!"

Mason blinked at her. "Uh . . . congrats?"

Louisa huffed, clearly not happy with that response. She flipped her tablet back to her and started scrolling through it, keeping her eyes on the screen as she continued, "It was a bit of a last minute event, but we managed to pull it together. All the proceeds will help fund this year's annual Children's Dinner—it's a banquet we host for a number of children from our donation program and their families."

"That's cool," Mason said, hoping that if he kept up his responses he could slowly return to playing his game. He picked up his controller, keeping his eyes on Louisa as she continued to tap away at her tablet.

"And, well, I hadn't really thought about this at first," she went on, "but, now that you're here, I figured it would be perfect!"

"Hmm?" His thumb was hovering over the 'play' button.

"Here it is!" She held up the tablet once again. The screen displayed a web page for the event. At the top of the page were the words friends and family invited! "Everyone from the foundation who is going will bring their kids. So, I just thought, if you wanted to . . ."

*Ice cream social?* Mason thought. *'Friends and family?' Yeah, the last thing I want to do is spend the day with a bunch of little kids covered in ice cream.*

"Thanks, Louisa, but I don't know. Aren't I kind of old to go to something like that?"

"Oh." Her shoulders slumped. "Yes, I guess so. Right. Sorry—I suppose I need to get used to being the parent of a teenager, don't I?" She let out a forced laugh.

She started walking out of his bedroom, and Mason took that as a go ahead to start playing his game again. "Lord Pembrooke had mentioned he was going to bring his daughter to help out, so I just figured . . . Well, never mind. You're probably right anyway. I won't drag you to some silly children's event."

*Lord Pembrooke . . . wait a minute—Brianna will be there?* Mason paused the game again, but Louisa had already left the room. "Louisa? Hey wait—Louisa! Okay, fine, I'll go!"

\*\*\*

Balloons were tied to nearly every streetlight, bench, and fence at the park where the ice cream social was held. A kids' band played on a small stage, and there were several costumed characters taking photos with kids. Most of the people there were adults or children, so Mason kept an eye out for Brianna—likely the only other teenager at the event.

"Oh, there's the ice cream booth," Louisa said. "It looks great!"

He followed her gaze across the park to where several tables were clustered together to form a giant ice cream assembly line. Families were lined up to grab a bowl, select an ice cream flavor, and choose from a variety of toppings. Standing in the center of the assembly line was Brianna, wearing a little apron and working the sprinkle station.

"Hey, um, I'm gonna get in line," Mason said, hoping his voice sounded casual. But Louisa's attention had already been grabbed by someone else, and she waved him off, telling him she'd meet up with him later.

As he approached, he watched Brianna smile at child after child, giving them a healthy pour of colorful sprinkles on top of their mound of ice cream. She clearly had a knack for outreach work like this.

*Okay*, he told himself. *Think of something clever to say.*

The next kid in line was struggling to choose between strawberry and chocolate ice cream, so Mason took the opportunity to slide up to Brianna's station. She was wiping off the tabletop, so she didn't notice him right away.

Mason leaned a hip on the table across from her, hoping he looked laid back. "Got any . . . extra sprinkles?"

*GAH! What is the matter with you?* he immediately thought to himself with a cringe. Even the kid ahead of him gave him a weird look.

"Um, what?" Brianna snorted, her gaze still down. When she finally looked up at him, her face shifted in recognition. "Oh, hey!" She smiled. "Sorry—I thought you were a creep or something. I'm glad it was just you. Real funny."

Mason tried to give a casual laugh, but it turned out more like a weird something-stuck-in-your-throat noise. "Oh, yeah, I was—I was just messing with you." He cleared his throat.

By now Chocolate-Versus-Strawberry Kid had chosen and was staring at them expectantly. Mason stepped back so Brianna could pour some sprinkles on top of the already monstrous scoop of ice cream. When the kid moved on to the next station, Mason stepped closer again.

"So you got stuck working at this thing, huh?" he asked.

Brianna glanced away. "I volunteered, actually. It's fun to go to all these different events, and I like helping people."

He nodded hastily. "Yeah, definitely. Cool." *Brianna's a joiner, you idiot*, he scolded himself. *She's not gonna be the type to complain about working events like this.*

Before he could attempt to steer the conversation in another direction, Brianna looked up at him again. "Do you want an ice cream or something?" She subtly gestured to the build-up of expectant children that were gathering because he was blocking the way. Kids were downright glaring at him for holding up the line.

"Oh—nah, I'm good. Thanks. I'll see you later." He made one last attempt—giving her a crooked smile that he may or may not have practiced in the mirror. But Brianna had already moved on to the next child in line.

Mason huffed and stepped away from the line. He was about to wander off and find somewhere to sit for the rest of the event when he noticed someone down the line approach a volunteer and say, "Shift's over. I'll take over for you!"

Mason found Louisa standing off to the side with a photographer. "Hey, I was wondering if you guys needed any extra volunteers," he said when he approached her.

Louisa beamed at that. "That is so kind of you! We had hoped for a few extra signups in the cleanup crew—"

"Actually," Mason cut in before his whole plan went out the window and he found himself assigned to cleanup for the rest of the afternoon. "I was thinking I could help with the ice cream booth."

Louisa looked surprised.

"Yeah, uh, I just heard a guy say he could use a break," he added quickly, gesturing behind him.

"That's great! Let's get you an apron." She excitedly led the way to a truck filled with supplies. Apparently each of the volunteers at the ice cream booth had to wear an apron and a pair of gloves. Certainly not the best outfit for him to talk to Brianna in, but it could be worse—he could be carrying a trash bag and smelling like garbage.

On one side of Brianna was the actual ice cream to be scooped, but that felt like way too much pressure. Plus he had no interest in dealing with indecisive kids who couldn't choose between flavors. On the other side of her was a station with a variety of toppings— nuts, mini marshmallows, crumbled cookies.

He stepped up to the man working that station and said, "Hey, I can take over."

The man looked rather confused but took the opportunity for the break anyway. Mason carefully stepped up to the station and began straightening out the bins of toppings, as if he'd completely forgotten Brianna was working right next to him.

"So you're behind the booth now," she said, clearly seeing right through his actions. He couldn't help but like that about her.

Mason shrugged. "What can I say? I'm passionate about ice cream."

She laughed and rolled her eyes. "Sure you are."

They didn't say anything to each other for a while as kids one after another came through the line for their ice cream toppings. Brianna chatted with the kids as they passed, making jokes and seeing how high she could hold the scooper while still getting the sprinkles into their bowls. Soon Mason found himself loosening up as well.

Slowly the line started to thin out. The

last girl in line was the youngest he'd seen yet, her head barely poking above the table. She held her bowl above her head in tiny hands, refusing to let her parents help her. She politely asked for sprinkles and then mini marshmallows. Mason bent down and playfully analyzed her bowl as if he were making sure she had just the right amount of marshmallow coverage. "Okay, I think you're good," he said, and the girl giggled. When he looked up, Brianna was watching him and trying to hide a smile.

His stomach flipped, but he tried not to let himself overthink it. He smirked at her and she looked away. "Can I help you?" he said teasingly.

She blushed, keeping her gaze down and fiddling with her apron. "I don't know what you're talking about."

"Uh-huh, whatever you say, Bri."

"It's *Brianna*." She tossed her rag at him and the grin on her face grew. Then she glanced around. There was no line for the ice cream now, and everyone seemed to be happily eating and mingling. "Looks like we're not needed here anymore . . ."

*She's leaving?* He was flooded with disappointment. Mason glanced around, scratching at the back of his head. "Yeah, guess so."

Brianna nodded, taking off her apron and folding it up slowly. He watched as she held it in her hands for another moment before she finally set it on the table. "So, I guess I'll see you later then."

There was a very good chance she genuinely meant that. She may have just had fun goofing around with him for the last hour and wasn't interested in anything more. But she seemed to linger now. Mason decided it was worth one more chance.

"Or," he said, feeling a little shy this time, "we could keep hanging out. If you wanted. I mean, we're kind of the only young people here who aren't about to get our faces sticky with ice cream."

Brianna laughed. "You say that now," she said, "but volunteers get a free scoop . . ."

8

After they'd each gotten their ice cream—
carefully analyzed by Mason to ensure
their bowls also had a decent coverage of
mini marshmallows—they took a seat on
a bench away from the crowd. Brianna
sighed contentedly as she lifted her spoon to
her mouth.

"You really *do* like all this stuff, don't you?"
Mason asked her, gesturing around the park
with his spoon.

"Like I said, I like helping people—and I'm
not just saying that because it looks good on an
application," she said. "I always enjoyed going
to events with my father when I was little, and
then . . ." She lowered her bowl to rest on her

legs, and Mason could tell the conversation was taking a turn.

"My little sister was diagnosed with cancer when she was a toddler."

"Oh, wow, I'm sorry."

"She's been in remission for several years now."

"That's great," Mason said.

"It's amazing." Brianna nodded. "I've been interested in children's health research ever since. It's so important." She smiled shyly then and said, "I've really enjoyed watching Louisa and her work with the foundation. She's so inspiring."

Mason turned to her. "Have you told her that? I bet she'd let you work for her."

"Oh, I don't really know her, actually. We've been introduced but that's it."

"I can put in a good word for you if you want."

Brianna blinked at him in surprise. "Really? You'd do that?"

"Sure." He stood up. "Let's go."

"Right now?" she asked, trailing after him.

"Yeah, right now. C'mon—she'll be happy to chat with you."

As they headed toward Louisa, Mason tried not to smile at the way Brianna nervously combed her fingers through her hair and straightened out her shirt.

"Louisa," he called, gesturing for her to join them. "You've met my friend, Brianna Pembrooke."

"Brianna, thank you so much for helping out today." Louisa grinned at her.

Brianna beamed. "It was a pleasure, Your Grace. I was just telling Mason that working at events like this is so much fun. And I really appreciate the work you do." She continued on about the events she's seen the foundation put on, and Louisa sent Mason a knowing look, clearly hiding her amused smile.

"You should consider applying for an internship with us when you're ready," Louisa said when Brianna was finished. "We'd be happy to have you."

"Oh my gosh, thank you. I would love that."

Louisa began to respond, but before Mason even knew what was happening he was opening his mouth and saying, "And in the meantime, we should organize an event for the foundation together before I leave."

If he was being honest, he didn't exactly mean it. But Brianna and Louisa both looked positively thrilled by this idea and immediately began to discuss plans. Mason couldn't get another word in.

*** 

The next morning when he came downstairs for breakfast, Mason was surprised to hear a familiar voice in the study. He rounded the corner and found Louisa sitting with Brianna at a small table, each of them typing away at laptops. He'd never been more thankful that he didn't wander around in his boxers in the morning.

"Bri? What are you doing here?"

"Hi, Mason," she said cheerfully. "You're late! We've been discussing our charity event for twenty minutes."

Mason glanced at the half-empty cups of tea sitting on the table. "Late? It's, like, nine o'clock . . ."

Louisa gestured for him to sit with them. "We've decided, since it was your idea, that you should be the one to choose what type of event we put on."

"Oh, you guys don't have to do that. I'm cool with doing whatever you want—"

"Come on, Mason," Brianna said. "I'm sure you can think of something."

Mason lowered himself into a chair, wishing he'd at least gotten in a cup of coffee before having to turn on his brain like this. They both stared at him expectantly, and it was clear that they were not going to let up on this. He scrambled to come up with an idea that might actually be interesting to him. "I guess . . . uh, what about something with music?"

"Music?" Louisa nodded, turning back to her laptop and already beginning to type rapidly. He had no idea what she possibly could have gotten off of just that, but apparently that was enough to get her off and running.

"What kind of music?" Brianna asked.

"Maybe a concert where the proceeds go to the foundation?" Then he sat up. "Yeah, a concert with local bands. Nathan plays in one—I bet he can tell us about some others too. They'll be more likely to play at the last minute like this. And they'll be cheap—they'll probably play just for the exposure."

"I love it," Louisa said, grinning.

"So do I!" Brianna added.

Louisa continued typing. "I'm sure there are a few concert venues that would be available on short notice—especially for a good cause."

Mason felt like he was watching a tennis match between Louisa and Brianna, who was now typing away at her laptop as well. He wondered if he was supposed to be typing something too. Then he came up with another idea. "We could invite kids with illnesses and their families. Maybe have a free section for them."

Brianna paused at that, turning to him with a look in her eye he'd never seen before. Mason felt his cheeks heat up under the intensity of her stare, and he noticed Louisa smiling in amusement again, though she kept her gaze on her screen. He coughed. "I mean, if you wanna do that."

"Absolutely," Brianna breathed.

Mason heard a throat clear behind him and turned to see his dad standing in the doorway with two mugs of coffee in his hands. "Already getting to work I see."

"Mason had the greatest idea, Mr. Everett," Brianna said. She began listing off potential concert locations to Louisa, who nodded along eagerly.

Mason's dad handed him a mug of coffee and raised his own in salute. Mason raised his back before taking a sip. For the first time since he could remember, he was actually excited to be part of something.

9

Over the next three weeks, Mason, Brianna, and Louisa worked to organize their charity concert. They managed to find a small theater that could fit them in two nights before Mason and his dad were supposed to return home.

Louisa had her staff at the foundation helping as well, but she trusted Mason and Brianna to handle most of the preparations. Nathan and Cora were helping too. They'd each been drawn to different aspects of planning the event—Nathan recruited and coordinated the bands; Cora, who enjoyed writing, drafted and reviewed all written communication; and Brianna took a natural role at Louisa's side as event organizer. Mason was even surprised at how much he'd enjoyed getting involved. He didn't quite have one area where he preferred to work, but he found he actually liked being involved in a little bit of everything.

What he liked most of all, though, was that Brianna was coming around the house nearly every day at this point. Mason found himself excited to get out of bed in the morning.

"Just wait until you try these pastries," she said to him eagerly one morning. They'd been trading off on providing breakfast for several days now. Brianna held up the box she'd brought. "They're an Evonian specialty—no one else makes them."

"I'm always down to try a new form of doughnut." He followed her down the hall toward the garden, where they usually worked if the weather allowed.

"You're so American," she teased. "These are *better* than doughnuts."

Mason grabbed her shoulders and pretended to give her a serious look. "*Nothing* is better than doughnuts."

Brianna made a show of rolling her eyes, though he noticed her cheeks get a little pink. They stepped away from each other and continued outside.

Out of the corner of his eye, Mason spotted his dad and Louisa trying to hide their smiles. Neither of them had said anything to him about Brianna, although they certainly gave each other plenty of knowing looks. Mason pretended not to notice.

Nothing had happened between him and Brianna yet. But that was just fine with Mason. And besides, he had a plan.

*  *  *

After a long day of finalizing details, Cora, Nathan, and Brianna were heading out for the night. The concert was just three days away, and nearly everything was finished.

Mason walked them out the front door and paused in the front entryway, grabbing Brianna's arm. "Hey, wait a second, Bri."

She stopped, looking at him in surprise. Over her shoulder, he could see Nathan and

Cora continuing down the drive, though they'd turned and were now giving him the thumbs up. Mason shook his head at them, trying to clear his focus.

"I, uh . . ." he glanced down at his feet hesitantly. He was more nervous than he thought he'd be. "Well, you know the concert is coming up soon, and I've had a lot of fun spending time with you planning it."

She smiled, and his heart began to pound. "So have I."

"And, I guess . . . I was just wondering if you'd want to go with me to the concert. Like, as my date."

Her eyes lit up with excitement. "I would love to."

Mason grinned. "Awesome."

Then she kept looking up at him expectantly. He took a step closer, reaching for her hand and leaning toward her.

And then the front door opened behind them.

Mason and Brianna jumped away from each other as his dad stared at them from the doorway. "Oh. Hey. I was just coming to see where you went."

"I was just saying goodbye to Brianna," Mason said hastily, taking another step away from her.

He waved at her melodramatically. "So . . . goodbye."

"Yes. Right. Good night, Mason. Good night, Mr. Everett." Brianna looked mortified as she turned quickly and sped down the walkway to where Nathan and Cora were waiting.

They watched the car pull away, and Mason's dad cleared his throat.

"Shut up," Mason mumbled, brushing past his dad to get inside.

He could just *hear* the smile in his dad's voice. "I wasn't gonna say anything."

**10**

Over the next couple days, Louisa and
Mason's dad seemed to share secret glances
whenever Mason would come into the room.
He had a feeling his dad told her about the
doorway mishap.

But the night before the concert, Louisa
made an announcement. "Your father and
I have a surprise for you. We've arranged
for your friends to fly in and come see the
show tomorrow."

At first, Mason didn't know who she was
talking about. He immediately thought of
Cora, Nathan, and Brianna. Then he realized
she'd actually meant Chase and Andre. "Wow,
that's—wow, Louisa. Thanks."

Now his parents' secretive looks made more sense. They'd been planning this together. At least it was a better surprise than the other secrets they'd kept from him over the years.

Chase and Andre arrived early in the afternoon the next day, so he had time to bring them to the house and show them around town before the concert. After introducing them to Louisa, Mason led them up to his bedroom.

"Dude, your room is awesome," Andre said, plopping back on the bed.

"Do you get to keep all this stuff when you come home?" Chase asked. He was looking through the stacks of video games that Mason had forgotten about over the past few weeks. He'd been so busy with Louisa and his new friends that he didn't spend much time in his room anymore.

"I guess so," Mason said. "I haven't really thought about it."

Chase snorted. "Please. If I were you, I'd never leave this room."

Mason shrugged. "Yeah, well, I've been really busy helping Louisa with this concert.

And my friends here have been too. We don't really spend much time in my room."

"So, what is this concert thing?" Andre asked. "Like a battle of the bands?"

"Not really. Local bands are performing, but it's for a charity event for Louisa's foundation."

His friends looked over at him doubtfully, and Mason didn't like it. "What?"

"*You?* Charity work?" Chase teased. "Yeah, right."

"What's that supposed to mean?"

"Come on, man," Andre said. "You know you're not exactly the 'go-getter' type."

He didn't know why he suddenly felt so defensive. "Yeah, well, it's not that bad. I mostly hang out with my friends, Nathan and Cora. And Brianna."

"Oh, there we go," Andre said with a grin. "So there's a girl."

"It's not like that," Mason insisted. "I mean, it sort of was at first. But—it's different. This is important to my mom too."

"Yeah sure, bud," Chase said. He turned

to Andre. "No wonder he hasn't messaged us all month—between this sweet setup and a hot Evonian girl, I wouldn't ever want to leave either."

His friends laughed, but Mason felt a churning in his stomach. He didn't like the way they talked about Brianna, even though he used to talk like that about other girls back home. But he especially didn't like the way they talked about him.

11

By the time they'd all gotten dressed for the
concert that night, Mason was wishing his
friends had never come to Evonia in the first
place. They'd goofed around all evening—
nothing different from the way they used
to hang out—but Mason found himself not
interested in their antics at the moment.

He was picking up Brianna at her place that
night—Cora too, since Nathan was already at
the theater with his band to warm up. While
offering to drive them had seemed like a good
idea at the time, now Mason regretted it. His
friends insisted on coming along to pick up
the girls, and it was clear as soon as the car
took off that the girls were not fans of Chase

and Andre. They spent the entire car ride calling the girls "milady" and pretending to offer them champagne in horrible attempts at Evonian accents.

Mason rolled his eyes. The guys thought they were being hilarious, while Cora and Brianna clearly did not. He caught Brianna's eye and tried to send her an apologetic look.

By the time they got to the theater, Mason was more than ready for the night to be over. Louisa introduced him to a few people, and every time he shook someone's hand he could hear his friends snickering in the background. Normally her introductions didn't bother him, but tonight Mason felt the back of his neck turn red each time.

Louisa was supposed to kick off the concert with a small welcome announcement. Their group had a row of seats in the balcony, and when she headed off to get onstage, Mason drifted over to his friends to bring them to their seats.

"Dude, you are such a puppet," Andre teased when he reached them.

"What?"

"A puppet," Chase said. "You're here doing whatever these people tell you to do. It's like we don't even know you anymore."

"That's not true," Mason insisted, although suddenly he found himself questioning it. He'd been enjoying himself these past few weeks here—hadn't he?

"Look, I'm sure it's weird with your mom," added Chase. "But you don't owe her anything, man."

Mason struggled to think of a response. Suddenly it was hard to tell if he'd really been having fun here, or if he'd just been trying to convince himself that he'd forgiven Louisa and everything was fine.

The sound of laughter caught his attention, and he spotted Louisa down the hall chatting with Brianna. He couldn't deny that he'd been doing a lot of this to get closer to Brianna, to impress her. Or at least, that's how it had started.

"And that girl *is* hot," said Andre. "But I don't think she's that into you. She seems more into your mom, actually."

Chase laughed. Mason was too stunned to react. He knew Andre was just joking, but he couldn't help but wonder . . . *Has she been pretending to be interested in me just to get closer to Louisa?*

After all, she'd known that Louisa was his mother from the start. His memories of the first night they met at the party, hanging out at the ice cream social, the time they spent together over the past few weeks were suddenly tainted. Had she really just wanted a shot at impressing Louisa? Something deep in Mason's gut twisted. His mind raced as he struggled to piece together what had been real and what hadn't.

Louisa stepped away from Brianna, who turned and smiled at him. Mason attempted to return the smile, but it didn't feel quite natural anymore. His friends seemed to notice this.

"C'mon, man," Chase said, "let's get out of here."

"What?" Mason turned back to them.

"Let's ditch this thing," Andre said. They moved down the hall leading to the front doors, gesturing for Mason to follow.

He hesitated, uncertain of what he should do. His friends and Louisa had worked so hard on this event. Part of him pointed out that he'd worked hard on it too. But Mason thought back to Brianna buddying up to Louisa, which caused prickling spitefulness to rise up in him. *None of it was real*, he told himself. *The guys are right—this place, these people have just been messing with me.*

Andre called to him, pulling him from his thoughts. Mason nodded and followed them.

"Mason?" Brianna called out. He could hear her chasing after him. He paused by the front door and stepped away from his friends.

"What are you doing?" Brianna asked, her eyes flicking over to them.

Aware that Andre and Chase were listening, Mason shoved his hands into his pockets. "What does it matter?" he asked. "You don't need me anymore—you got what you wanted. I'm getting out of here."

"What are you talking about?"

"My mom," he said. "You said so yourself, you've always admired what she did with

the foundation. You just needed an in
with her."

Brianna's jaw dropped. "That's *not* what
this is has been about."

"Whatever. It's not like I was planning on
staying for this thing anyway."

She stepped closer to him and lowered her
voice. "Mason," she pleaded, "what's wrong?"

"Nothing's wrong, except that I don't want
to waste my life sucking up to rich people.
Unlike you, I guess."

His friends tried to hide their snorts
of laughter.

She shot a sharp glare at them before
turning back to him. "I know that this whole
'too cool to care about anything' bit you have
going on is just an act. I know you want to
do more with your life."

"You sound just like my parents," he said,
rolling his eyes. "So worried about whether or
not I'll go to college after high school."

"It's not about going to college—I don't
care what you want to do after high school.
Get a job, explore the world, whatever. It's just

about doing *something*—having goals, wanting to contribute to the world."

Mason didn't know what to say to that. Not with his friends watching.

Brianna reached for one of his hands and held it in hers. "Please," she said. "Don't leave. This is important to me. I know it is to you too."

"Oh, like you really know anything about me," snapped Mason. Brianna yanked her hand from his and stormed back down the hall.

Mason sighed and took a step in her direction. He hadn't meant to sound so harsh, and part of him truly wanted to stay. "Hold on, Bri—"

She whipped around, narrowing her eyes at him. "*Don't* call me that."

As she continued down the hall, his friends burst into laughter.

"Jeez, that girl is uptight," Chase said. His friends laughed again, but Mason could only clench his jaw. He didn't know what else to do besides follow his friends out the doors.

They stepped outside to hail a taxi. A car pulled up, and as they climbed in, Cora rushed outside. Mason rolled down the window by his seat.

"Mason!" she called breathlessly. "Where are you going? Nathan's about to go on."

*Oh no*, he thought to himself, having completely forgotten about his friend's band. He hesitated once again. Before he could make a decision, the car was pulling away from the curb and taking them into the street. Mason mouthed an 'I'm sorry' to Cora, who simply watched him from the sidewalk.

**12**

Mason and his friends returned to the house late, having spent the rest of the night traveling around town and goofing off. It had been fun to hang out with Andre and Chase again, although Mason couldn't shake the guilt he felt.

They crept quietly into the house. His friends sneaked up the stairs to their bedrooms in the guest wing, and Mason breathed a sigh of relief—everyone was already in bed.

And then his dad and Louisa stepped out from the study.

"In," his dad snapped, waving a hand toward the study.

Mason slumped into a large armchair and waited for the lecture to begin.

"I cannot believe what you did tonight," his dad started. "Why would you just leave like that?"

Before Mason could respond, Louisa jumped in.

"Brianna told me about your argument," Louisa said. "How could you say those things to her?"

"Oh, whatever," Mason snapped. "She was just using me anyway."

"That's ridiculous," his dad said. "Brianna is a sweet girl, and she clearly cares about you. Why else would she be over here all the time? If she'd only wanted to get to know Louisa, she could've had her father arrange that. Do you really think she needed your help to impress your mom?"

Mason scowled, crossing his arms and slouching even further in his seat. He didn't know how to answer that. Earlier this evening, everything his friends were saying had made perfect sense. But once he was back here, he started questioning things all over again.

Louisa pressed her fingers between her eyebrows. "I came back from starting the show to find Brianna furious. Not to mention that Cora was upset that you had just run off without telling anyone where you were going. And *she* was the one who had to tell Nathan that you'd left before he'd even gone on."

Mason felt his stomach twist.

"I just don't see how you could be so irresponsible," Louisa continued. "Do you really care that little about the people who care about you? Or the things you do in your life?"

Something in Mason snapped. He knew he'd messed up tonight. But he'd had enough of his parents lecturing him on right and wrong. Not when he was in this entire situation because of them.

He stood up, clenching his fists. "You know what—you can't say anything to me about this. You haven't been in my life for the past seventeen years. What makes you think you can suddenly just swoop in and tell me what to do?"

Louisa was stunned into silence, but his dad wasn't. "Mason," he began very slowly, his voice in a deep tone of warning, "you cannot just—"

"You're no better either," Mason said over him. He waved an angry hand at the two of them. "You both did this. You two have made all the decisions in my life—it's not like I've had any say. Didn't you think about how this might affect me?"

This time they were both silent, the anger in their faces transitioning into guilt. His dad took a step forward. "Mason—"

"No!" he cut him off again. "You've lived with me all this time. You watched me grow up, knowing someday this would happen. It didn't once occur to you to tell me about her sooner than my seventeenth birthday?"

His dad rubbed at his face. "I wanted to tell you—I just didn't know how."

"There's nothing you can say to excuse what you guys did. How could you think I would want to go eighteen years without seeing my mother, without knowing anything about her? How was *this*," he waved his hands around wildly, "the best possible scenario you were able to come up with?"

It was as if all the tension in the air had been released. All the anger and confusion that had been building up in Mason since he'd first learned about his mother was finally coming out.

Quietly, his dad said, "I'm not trying to make excuses, Mason. Now's not the time for excuses . . . from any of us."

Mason sank back down into the chair, deflated. He couldn't blame his parents' mistakes for his own actions. When he thought back to how he'd let Chase and Andre guide his choices tonight, all his ideas about not being a follower felt pretty hollow.

"I know I screwed up tonight," he said then. "I shouldn't have left. I shouldn't have let my friends talk me into thinking I wasn't happy here. And I know I disappointed you. I disappointed Nathan. I got into a stupid fight with Brianna."

He looked up at them and felt his throat tighten. "But I've been so confused lately. I feel like I don't know who I am anymore."

Finally Louisa spoke again, tears gathering in her eyes. "Mason, sweetheart, I wish I could tell you something to make it better. We made a mistake—you're right. It was a stupid decision. We were young and scared and had no idea what to do. I'm so sorry. I'm sorry we made such a poor decision and I'm sorry it took us seventeen years to figure that out."

Mason nodded, not sure he could say anything else just yet.

"I'm sorry too," his dad said, wiping at his wet eyes. "I should have thought about what this might do to you. I thought I was looking out for you, but I screwed up."

Mason let out a long sigh. He understood that his parents had never meant to hurt him. There was no way to redo the past seventeen years—he knew that. But maybe this was what they all needed. They had to let everything out in order to get a clean start. It was something at least.

For the first time since he'd arrived in Evonia, Mason began to feel settled.

"Look," Louisa said quietly, "I know I haven't been there for you. But I hope I can make it up to you—for the rest of your life. I want to actually *be* your mother. You can come here whenever you'd like, or I'll come see you in the States. Whatever you want."

Mason nodded, taking in a shaky breath. "I'd like that."

His dad stepped forward. "We're here for you—both of us." Louisa clasped his dad's hand, and Mason watched as they shared a soft smile.

"That's all I want," Mason said. He met Louisa's eyes. "I just want my mom in my life."

She burst into tears again. He stepped closer and Louisa wrapped her arms around his shoulders. It was the first time she'd really hugged him, but it was amazing how right it felt.

Mason closed his eyes and leaned into her. Their family situation was unusual—and maybe it would always be unusual. But at least the three of them were now in this together.

"I love you, sweetheart," she said quietly, squeezing her arms.

He squeezed back. "Love you too . . . Mom."

13

The first thing Mason did when he woke up the next morning was send his friends home. They would always be his friends, but Mason could see now that they didn't fit with this new version of himself. And he liked this version of himself. Maybe down the road he'd be able to mend things with them again, but for now he wanted to focus on repairing things here.

He'd made up with his parents, but he knew there was still a lot he needed to do. He couldn't leave without fixing things with his new friends. And Brianna. He didn't know *what* they were exactly, but he knew she was more than just a friend to him.

He started with Nathan, who lived within walking distance. Mason wandered into the yard behind Nathan's house until he heard the soft strumming of an acoustic guitar. He found Nathan and Cora sitting together in a gazebo. They both turned at the sound of his footsteps, and Nathan stopped strumming.

"Hey," Mason said quietly, shoving his hands into his pockets. Nathan gave a quick nod in response, while Cora said nothing. But they didn't turn him away. Mason took that as a go ahead to come into the gazebo with them.

"I came to say I'm sorry. I was confused with a lot of stuff that's been going on. My friends were saying all these things and I got into a fight with Bri and . . . well, I guess that's no excuse for ditching—"

"No, it's not," Cora said.

Mason sighed. "Yeah. I was a huge jerk and I know it and I'm sorry." He turned to Nathan. "I left before you got to play, and that sucks. But I'll make it up to you however I can."

Nathan was quiet for a moment. He glanced at Cora, then he turned back to

Mason, giving him a wide grin. "Okay. I forgive you."

Mason let out a laugh of relief. "Jeez, I thought you were gonna, like, shun me or something."

"I thought about it, but I figured it would be easier to know I can crash at your place if I ever want to come see a concert in the States," Nathan teased.

"Absolutely," Mason said.

"And you'll have to come back and see us perform some other time."

"Totally." Mason nodded enthusiastically. "I'd love to. I'll be right in the front row, screaming so loud it's embarrassing."

They laughed again, and this time Cora joined in. "Okay," she said. "I guess I can forgive you too then." Mason grinned.

"So," Nathan continued, "you making your rounds with apologies?"

Mason groaned. "My mom and dad really tore into me last night. But it ended up being good—I think we all needed to let it out. We talked about a lot."

"Well, I'm glad you're back to your normal self again," Cora teased. "Because we like you. So now you need to go make things better with Brianna so we can all go back to being friends."

Nathan nodded in agreement. "Yeah, have you talked to her yet?"

"Not yet," Mason said, not bothering to hide the dread in his voice. "I figured if you guys forgave me you might give me some advice on what to say to her. She won't answer any of my calls or texts."

"Well," Cora said mischievously, "I happen to know where she is."

\*\*\*

It turned out Brianna had a favorite park where she liked to go when she was upset. Mason figured last night certainly met the criteria. Cora had texted him directions to where Brianna usually sat, and he spotted her sitting on a bench with her arms wrapped around her bent legs and her chin resting on her knee.

"Hey," he called softly as he walked over to her.

She lifted her head in surprise. "Hi."

"Can I sit?" He nodded at the bench, and she slid over so he could join her.

They turned to each other and started speaking at the same time. Mason blinked at her in confusion, not expecting her to try to say something first. Brianna smiled sheepishly. "You were a jerk last night—if that's what you're here to say, I'm not going to stop you."

Mason barked out a laugh in surprise. This was not how he'd expected the conversation to begin.

"But," she said, staring out ahead of them, "I've been thinking a lot about what you said last night. About me."

"Look, Brianna, that wasn't—"

"I think you were a little right," she continued over him. "I knew you were Louisa's son when we first met, and I was interested in meeting her. So, maybe I did want to be friends with you because of that. But just at first."

She turned to him. "And then we worked at the ice cream social together, and I had so much fun with you. I felt like I could completely be myself around you. I thought you felt the same about me . . ."

"I did," Mason said, reaching for her hands. "Honestly, I did. Being here has made me see things differently. Getting to know my mom, getting to know you . . . it makes me want to do better, to get more out of my life. And then my friends came into town, and that just made everything confusing. They're good guys, but they're also a bunch of idiots. They tried to tell me I wasn't being myself anymore. But really, I like the kind of person I became while I've been here. I was a jerk last night, and I'm really sorry for it."

"It was like you were a completely different person," she admitted. "So if that's the real you, then you'd better tell me now."

"It's not," he insisted. "I don't want it to be."

"So, everything else . . . the way you were these past few weeks with me . . ."

"I'm not exactly used to being this guy,"

Mason admitted. "I've never been much of a . . . 'tryer.' But I like the way I am here."

"So do I," she said softly. They grinned at each other, and then Mason leaned toward her. He kissed her gently, bringing an arm around her shoulders as she moved closer.

When they pulled away, he kept his arm around her. "Who knows, maybe I'll come out here for college."

She shrugged. "Or maybe I'll go out to the States."

"Either way, Brianna."

She leaned her head toward him. "I thought it was Bri?" she asked with a teasing smile.

"Bri," he said, leaning in for another kiss.

14

During his last two days in Evonia, Mason split his time between his parents and his new friends.

He, Brianna, Nathan, and Cora had scheduled video chats to keep in touch every few weeks. Brianna and Cora were already making plans for the three of them to come visit Mason that winter. And Nathan had given him strict instructions to send email updates on the state of American rock music.

Though his dad wouldn't let him get an international phone plan, Mason and Brianna could still talk online whenever they wanted. He knew that this might not work out between them—long distance was hard enough when two people were in the same country. But they agreed to stay in touch and see what happened.

Things with Louisa, at least, were a little more certain. They would video chat weekly and had plans to swap holiday visits between Evonia and the US. They were also discussing doing some counseling sessions online to help all three of them.

On Mason's last night, Louisa had his friends over for dinner. "You know," Louisa said to him while the others were chatting at the other end of the table, "I'll understand if you want to stay in the States after you graduate high school."

He shrugged, looking at both of his parents. "I'm not really sure yet, but I'll think about it. One thing I do know is that I'd like to spend some time out here after I graduate, just to get to know this side of my background better. We'll see what happens then."

"I can't wait," Louisa said.

Mason smiled in agreement. "Neither can I."

**LOREN BAILEY** is a writer and editor in Minneapolis, Minnesota. She enjoys adventuring, baking, binge-watching Netflix, and spending too much time on the internet. *Becoming Prince Charming* is her debut novel.